INVADING UNIVERSE

ALL WORLDS COLLIDE

BY

JONAH JAMES

Library of Congress Catalog Number: 2024925344
James, Jonah
Invading Universe
ISBN 978-1-7357296-1-9 (paperback)

Publisher Information:
Cross City Creations
Walnut, Mississippi 38683
www.crosscitycreations.com

CONTENTS

HOUSE HORRORS
CHAPTER 1

On planet Tywer, a man was adventuring through his house when he heard a creak behind him.

He turned around and saw something, but he couldn't make out what it was. He rubbed his eyes, and when he opened them again, it was gone. He decided to go back to bed, but as he was almost asleep, he heard another creak at the door. He decided not to care and went to bed anyway.

He woke up at 5:00 in the morning and got ready for work. He got in his car, and before he left, he saw it again. He still couldn't make out what it was, so he decided to ignore it again. He arrived at his workplace, a restaurant, and found it there once more. He was tired of seeing that thing. He went to confront the creature and ask it to leave the restaurant, but as soon as he touched it, it vanished.

That night, he began packing and preparing to move to another house. But he couldn't stop wondering what the creature was, so he decided to stay a few more nights. He eventually figured out its weakness and decided to see if he could catch it that night. He told himself that if he messed up, he would die, but he hoped to at least get a picture of the haunting ghost.

He stayed up all night, waiting and waiting. It was 2:32 AM when he heard a noise. A few minutes later, he saw it again. This time, he led it into the trap. It got tangled in ropes. The man got a closer look at it, examining and testing to see if it was dangerous. Then, out of nowhere, an explosion happened, scaring him. He ran into the house, grabbed everything he could, and ran out.

While driving, he saw the creature behind him, angrier than before and running faster. The man sped up, but the faster he drove, the faster it ran. He tried to run it over, but once it was under the car, it tore through the metal. It emerged from the bottom of the car. The man jumped out the car window and kept the car rolling.

The car crashed into a tree. Fortunately, he survived. He ran to his neighbor's house and knocked frantically on the door. But the creature had other plans. It killed him, and the neighbor witnessed the whole thing. The neighbor was traumatized—but little did anyone know, it was the neighbor who had created the monster.

THE INVESTIGATION INCREASE

CHAPTER 2

Someone had to stop the neighbor, and the police couldn't figure out who had killed the man. Then a woman decided to solve the mystery. Her name was Amanda Coltas, and she began investigating the area around the body. She found an ax stuck in a tree and also spotted something nearby. Upon closer inspection, it turned out to be a squirrel.

Amanda decided to leave for the night but returned early the next morning to continue her investigation. She started with the body. There were no visible scratches or wounds on him, and she wondered, "How did he die if there's no damage to the body?" After some thought, she realized the monster that had killed him had done so with its mind. Just then, she heard something. She went to investigate and discovered the monster moving behind the house.

She quietly crept to the back of the house and found broken metal. Suddenly, she turned around—and was killed by the monster with a chair. The monster was incredibly intelligent, and no one knew who it really was. Perhaps, one day, they would find out.

The next day, the neighbor wondered if he had gone too far. He had killed two people. But then he heard banging on his door. When he opened it, the monster was standing there, listening to him. The creature burst through the door and ripped his head off. The monster was truly evil.

The following day, everyone in the city noticed a mysterious man walking the streets. At first, they didn't think anything was wrong. But when someone bumped into the man, he died instantly from the monster's gaze.

Soon, everyone began to stare at the monster. One man turned and ran, glancing back to see the monster right in front of him. How long would this nightmare continue? The monster nearly killed him in one bite. The rest of the people panicked and started driving away, but one of the cars exploded, sending metal shards and organs flying everywhere.

The man who had run away survived and kept running, knowing the monster wasn't human. He was the only one to escape. But what about

Amanda? She had to have survived if that man had made it through the monster's bite. She was running toward the city to warn everyone, but by the time she arrived, everyone was already dead.

Determined to find out what the creature was, Amanda and the man met up. He was a good friend of hers—they had graduated together. Together, they went inside and tried to figure out how the monster was created. They discovered that it wasn't a person in a costume; it was a black figure. No one knew what it was, but now they had a sense of what they were up against.

Amanda suggested that if they started a fire, the creature would get closer, and they could capture it. They tried the plan, and they succeeded in trapping the monster—but it broke free almost immediately. The two friends ran as fast as they could, seeking cover. While hiding, they thought of another plan.

"Surely this will work," they hoped.

This time, they laid down tar on the driveway, with a squirrel trapped in it. Their plan was to lure the monster to the tar and trap it there. They believed the tar was stronger than rope, so they were confident it would hold. They waited for the monster to appear, and when it came for the squirrel, they trapped it. The monster didn't know who had caught it, which worked to their advantage.

The next day, while waiting for the monster to show up, they continued their investigation. They still didn't know what species the monster was. However, they discovered its weakness: light. That's why it only came out at night—it was afraid of sunlight. This was a huge breakthrough for them. All they had to do now was get the monster into the light.

They planned to try it the next day, but overnight, the monster escaped. When they woke up, they found it had fled. "Since it's daylight, the monster is hiding," Amanda said. They began searching the city, but the monster was nowhere to be found. They went to a nearby town to ask people if they had seen it.

When they arrived, they found the town had been destroyed by the monster. They needed to figure out what happened between the attacks. They discovered that the monster didn't use its mind to kill after all. Instead, it used a weapon—an ax—rather than its hands.

They began working on a new plan to kill the monster, starting by trying to get hold of its weapon. They set up a trap where something heavy would fall, catching the monster off-guard. The idea was to steal the ax. However, they would have to wait for the right moment.

That night, they heard the monster approaching. Would their plan work? The creature walked straight into the trap, and the heavy object fell. The plan had worked, but now the monster was enraged and started chasing them. The next few minutes were absolutely terrifying as the monster pursued them, relentless and fast.

UNIVERSE PROTECTION SYSTEM
CHAPTER 3

The two grew tired and hid from the monster as it increased in size, becoming more terrifying than ever. They managed to sneak back to the lab unnoticed and quickly resumed their research on the creature. "Becomes bigger when angered, can't escape," they noted. They were never seen again.

On another planet, the inhabitants had sent a ship to study the monster. They discovered that the creature drew its power from the man's neighbor. The ship's crew began heading toward Earth, which appeared completely different than before. A few minutes later, a loud bang shook the ship. The guards rushed to find two giant holes in the hull. The ship began spinning out of control, and since they couldn't speak in space, they used a special language to communicate. They rebalanced the ship and repaired the holes, but when they looked back, Earth was gone.

They couldn't find the solar system anywhere. They checked the radar, but there was nothing. They wondered if the monster might be a planet eater. Before they could conclude anything, something popped up on the radar. "Stop…" it said, and then it changed to "tracking." The crew pondered what it meant. When they looked back, they saw a galaxy. Then, a huge chunk of it disappeared. They realized that the more the monster ate, the larger it grew.

Since the monster was black, it was nearly impossible to see in space, and it started devouring entire galaxies. Inside the monster was the solar system, and somehow, they were still alive. The man and the woman were inside, trying to figure out where they were. The monster was breathing loudly, and they looked around, desperately searching for an exit.

They noticed all the planets it had swallowed. The woman blamed herself for everything that had happened. The man tried to comfort her, saying it wasn't her fault. She disagreed, telling him it had been her idea to take the ax. Then the man saw the vastness of space—and, surprisingly, he found an exit! He warned the woman it would be a rough ride, but just then, the monster stopped breathing. They were suffocating inside.

They needed oxygen, and fast. They spotted a nearby dive bell and grabbed an oxygen tank. They tried to escape, but just as they reached the opening, the monster closed its mouth. They realized the creature was watching them very closely. They retreated, but then the monster opened its mouth again.

They quickly formed a new plan. One would go through one side of the monster, while the other went in the opposite direction. They decided to try the plan, but the monster wasn't paying attention to them. They tried screaming to get its attention, but it didn't work. Nothing seemed to work. In desperation, they looked around for anything that might grab the monster's focus—but they didn't realize they were running out of oxygen again. They had to act quickly.

They spotted a projectile that might be able to distract the monster, so they grabbed it and tried firing it. Unfortunately, it didn't get the creature's attention. They were running out of time—almost out of oxygen—and they died. There was no hope left for defeating the monster.

But the aliens who had been tracking the monster arrived. They saw how enormous the creature had grown, and they decided to retreat for the moment. They knew they needed a plan to defeat the monster, or the galaxies would be in grave danger. They began discussing strategies and formulating new plans.

After 30 minutes of planning, they had a solution. They were confident that this plan would work, no matter what. The idea was to send a decoy ship to approach the monster and distract it. While the monster was distracted, they would fire at its back. This would cause the part of the galaxy it had eaten to rejoin with the rest of the galaxy.

The decoy ship was destroyed by the monster, but it didn't seem to notice the aliens after that. They successfully freed the part of the galaxy the monster had swallowed, but the creature continued to eat. The aliens didn't have enough energy to shoot more lasers, so they switched to Plan B: using missiles to widen the crack they had made in the monster's back.

After another hour of missile fire, the crack grew larger. The monster kept eating and growing, fueled by the constant barrage of attacks. The aliens realized they needed to aim for the monster's heart to destroy it once and for all. They had only one missile left—one final chance.

The captain fired the missile, but it missed the heart. Knowing they had no other option, the crew rammed the ship into the monster's heart. The monster was killed, and the aliens became the heroes of the universe.

But the battle wasn't over. There were more of these monsters. Ship B-284392 had been destroyed, and all the crew inside perished. Another ship was sent to investigate, and the crew found the remains of B-284392 scattered across space. They discovered another massive monster approaching.

The aliens informed the mothership, which arrived in hyperspeed. The mothership had infinite energy reserves for its laser blasters, and they fired multiple shots at the creature. They quickly realized how B-284392 had been destroyed—the monster had grown immensely in size.

It had devoured the Andromeda galaxy before reaching the aliens. Now, it was enormous and still growing. The aliens fired their most powerful attack, and it opened the monster's head. They then targeted its brain, dealing significant damage. But the monster was furious.

HIDING HORROR
CHAPTER 4

The aliens were hiding from the monster, unaware of the full extent of its power. While they hid, they needed a plan to stop it. They came up with a few ideas that could work:

1. Distract it, get eaten, and destroy it from the inside.
2. Get it to chase the aliens while another ship destroys it from the back.
3. Use the Ultimate Power.

They hoped these plans would work, but they weren't sure if they were safe. They decided to try the first idea. Once they began, they started shooting everywhere in the monster's body. They spotted the heart but couldn't reach it in time. The ships J-240932 and K-284372 were destroyed in the process, but those were automated, computerized ships.

Next, they decided to try the second plan. They managed to get the monster's attention and shot at it from the back. The monster realized it was being attacked and turned around. Another ship began shooting from the opposite side. The monster became even angrier and took them down all at once.

How could anyone take down such a monstrous threat?

Desperate, they turned to the third plan: the Ultimate Power. They weren't sure if it would work, but they had no other choice. After a few minutes of flying toward the monster, they finally reached it. They unleashed the Ultimate Power, but they weren't sure it would be enough to bring the beast down. Miraculously, they didn't die in the process. The Ultimate Power was a combination of sodium combustion mixed with pericardial acid. It caused the monster to lose its front.

All they needed to do now was shoot the heart, with all the ships surrounding it. They began firing at the monster. The creature retaliated, destroying several of their ships. The monster was nearly impossible to defeat. Eventually, the monster killed them all. It seemed indestructible. Nothing could stop it. This was the greatest threat the universe had ever known.

If no one could stop it, entire multiverses would perish.

But just before the neighbor was killed, he secretly placed a special button in his pocket—one that would make the second monster die. The universe still had a chance. Someone had to press the button, but who?

The aliens were still alive, so all they needed to do was press it. That wouldn't be too hard… if only Tywer wasn't still inside the monster.

THE BIG PROBLEMS

CHAPTER 5

They began their journey toward the monster, which was mostly located in the Andromeda galaxy. They managed to get its full attention and angered it. They needed to wait for the right moment to attack because they only had one shot. When the time came, they took it and weakened the monster. They then entered the monster and found the correct house, carefully searching it from top to bottom.

They couldn't find the button, but the neighbor still had it in his pocket. Soon after, they located it, and they quickly exited the house and the monster. Once they were outside, they activated the button to destroy the second monster, bringing temporary peace. However, more monsters were on the way, and no one knew how to stop them.

A month passed, and a new monster appeared on the radar. They didn't know what to expect. It took the monster seven minutes to break through their defenses, and the crew was terrified. They fought back as best as they could, but the situation was dire. When the monster was finally killed, it took a chunk of the universe with it, just like the previous one. As the aliens fought the intruding monster, the universe itself was falling apart.

The aliens were unaware of the universe's collapse, still focused on fighting the monster. Once they finished, they noticed that stars were moving toward them. That's when they saw the universe was collapsing around them. Their first engine was hit, and they began losing control. Then the second, third, and fourth engines failed. They couldn't move at all and were left floating in space.

Hope was not entirely lost, though. They had other ships, and with them, they managed to push the damaged ship back to its starting point. They returned to their planet to repair it and get the engines working again. After a week, they had fixed one engine, but the ship was massive, and time was running out. The end of the universe was approaching quickly, and they had to work harder to catch up.

With the end of the universe so close, they put everyone aboard the ship and abandoned their planet. They were lucky this time, but they knew it wouldn't last forever. They traveled to the edge of the universe and stopped completely to conserve energy. The leader informed the crew that if they didn't leave the universe soon, their species would be doomed. They exited, only to discover that there were countless other universes, many of them far larger than their own.

THE NEW UNIVERSE
CHAPTER 6

The people were very pleased with the wide range of options available to them, but not everyone was happy. Some didn't share the optimistic view. They decided to explore a nearby universe called Arthearis, which contained many planets. They landed on one that was a wasteland, though the air wasn't toxic. From their vantage point, the only thing to fear was the heights. They realized they could live on a planet like this and start building a city. They imagined great things for their future city.

They got to work immediately and built a thriving city. Their currency was called tealites. They designed the city to function like a typical one, but with the added challenge of alien infestations. Despite the hardships, they were satisfied with their progress. However, some adventurous travelers decided to venture further and explore other parts of the world. Five of them left in the morning, but only two returned by 7:00 PM. We will explain why two came back, but first, let's look at the growth of the city.

They built much more on this planet than they had on their previous one. They constructed a station to monitor any potential threats near their world and focused on strengthening their defenses. Little did they know, monsters were already on their way. The explorers sent ships far into space and discovered other living creatures. They wanted to go further into Arthearis but were unable to, due to the monsters lurking nearby. On the planet Hearthiso, they discovered a new species called Endafs, a strange and unknown organism.

Realizing they needed to protect themselves, they began constructing machines for defense. They built a transformer, which lacked AI but had a driver's seat for manual control. They decided to travel to the planet where the Endafs had been discovered. Upon landing, they immediately noticed that the planet was different from their own. They set up cameras to scan for any signs of life. As they watched the feed, they saw the silhouette of a creature. Not knowing what it was, they decided to investigate.

This is where things took a dark turn for the travelers. As they got closer to the creature, it suddenly transformed into a monstrous form.

Terrified, they decided to leave it alone and return to their own planet. But when they arrived back, they saw the travelers—though something was very different about them. They appeared pale, almost zombie-like. Concerned, the inhabitants didn't want to let them inside without figuring out what had happened.

They had never encountered anything like this before, and fear spread quickly. The travelers suddenly burst through the door, and the people were terrified. The travelers created a crack in the wall and began forcing their way through it. The residents fought back, but they were nearly out of ammunition—amoxicillin, which was their standard weapon. In desperation, they switched to nanite acid, which seemed to work well for a time. However, their guns jammed.

They scrambled to fix the weapons before the travelers could break in. Eventually, the gun started working again, but when they fired, something strange happened—a hat was found inside the barrel. It had been placed there by one of the travelers. As the distraction worked, the travelers managed to get inside. The people watched in horror as the travelers began to painfully morph into a single, monstrous entity.

The creature tore the city apart, and everyone had to evacuate. In the end, the city was reduced to ruins.

"This universe isn't safe," the leader said seriously.

"We just got attacked by a monster," another person added.

SAFETY FIRST
CHAPTER SEVEN

They needed their ship, but it had been destroyed when the "travelers" attacked. They hoped it could still be repaired and that it would be able to fly again once fixed. Unfortunately, one of the wings was torn apart beyond repair. Luck wasn't on their side, and with no shelter left, they had to build a new ship. Luckily, they had materials from the old one. Two engineers worked tirelessly and built a new ship within two weeks.

This time, they installed more advanced weapons—laser slices, miniguns, and missiles. They were determined to be ready for anything. They gathered all the soldiers and set off for Hearthiso once again. Everyone was on high alert, prepared to fight. As they approached, they spotted one of the Endaf species. They immediately launched an attack. The creature emerged from the fog as a gnome-like being, only to transform into a monstrous form. The battle was fierce, and one of their ships was torn apart. They hadn't expected this. When they tried to retreat, the Endaf attacked the ship midair, causing more damage.

They managed to return to their planet and began rebuilding their city. The ships were sent to the mechanics for repairs. This time, however, they decided to prioritize defense over offense. They installed a one-way force field on the ships, giving them a better chance of survival. Once again, they went back to Hearthiso, only to find that the Endaf was waiting for them.

Suddenly, a chat bubble appeared, saying, "PLEASE BRING ME TO MEDALISTIC." It scanned the creature's face, but then the bubble flashed: "FACE AUTHORIZATION FALSE."

Confused, they left the planet, trying to figure out how to make the authorization true. A week passed, and one of the crew members discovered that a machine could create thousands of faces. They tried the idea, but the machine kept saying "authorization false." They realized they needed a bigger solution: find a person with authorization.

There were two options:

1. Spend years trying to find the right face.
2. Spend months searching the universe for someone who already had authorization.

They chose the second option for the sake of time. After three months of searching, they found a clue—footprints leading to a base. They followed them and found a human man sitting alone. They called for their ship to land quietly. As they approached him, the man suddenly pulled out a knife. Everyone backed away, but the man quickly pressed it to one of their necks.

"We mean no harm," the leader said.

They asked if the man had authorization to the Endafs. He replied, "I do, but these are very dangerous creatures, far beyond what you aliens can understand."

"We're willing to risk our lives to help," they insisted.

The man reluctantly agreed to help them. He led them back to the planet where the Endafs were. When they arrived, the machine scanned his face and said, "FACE AUTHORIZATION TRUE! WELCOME, JAXINO." The way was cleared for them to pass.

On the other side of the planet, there was a portal, but it wasn't accessible by ship. They began searching for the portal's entrance on foot. After days of searching, an alien member of the crew found a glowing rock. When they picked it up, a portal began to form before them. They called the others over to see, and soon everyone was gathered around. One of the crew members stepped through the portal and disappeared.

The rest followed, stepping into a new dimension. It was a strange and beautiful world, teeming with different creatures and life. However, not everything was peaceful. A large, shadowy presence loomed overhead, watching them closely. They froze in fear as they realized they were being observed.

One person bravely ventured forward, inspecting the world around them. He saw that it was vulnerable, perhaps weak. The team realized they had access to this world, so they brought their ships through the portal to gather resources. After returning to their planet, they used the new materials to strengthen their defenses.

They upgraded the defense towers and watchtowers, preparing for the inevitable monster attack. The people were nervous, but they were ready. As they waited, they saw strange visions. One saw a bull charging toward them, while another saw a bird, and yet another saw a ship. Each person saw something different, and paranoia began to set in. They were all on edge, unsure of what was to come.

The guards, though anxious, stayed vigilant. They sent soldiers into the wild to investigate, but they found nothing. The fear of the space monsters they had fought before still lingered. As they returned to the base, their fears grew. The tension was palpable—horrors seemed to be lurking just out of sight.

In a desperate attempt to face the unknown, they sent three fearless travelers to explore the wilds. Though scared, they embarked on their mission, sending photos back to the station. The travelers eventually found a suitable place to set up camp. After a day of exploration, they packed up and returned.

Despite the fear and uncertainty, they were pleased with what they had found—no monsters in sight. They were truly fearless explorers.

MONSTER MAYHEM
CHAPTER 8

Monsters were emerging from their hiding places. They noticed the people, and extinction seemed certain. Then, the aliens detected a heat signature up north. They sent soldiers to investigate and equipped them with heat-seeking missiles to track the source. They also added lasers to cut through space rocks. But that proved to be a mistake. The search began, and they soon encountered one of the monsters attempting to attack them. They defeated it quickly, but they knew an army would be a much greater challenge.

They had no idea what to expect. They thought they would be safe from the monsters, but the situation had changed. The monster from the neighbor's planet was still out there. The aliens didn't know much about this universe, and now monsters were showing up all over their radar. They hadn't noticed the danger until it was too late. The universe was no longer safe; it had become incredibly dangerous.

Monsters were now approaching the planet they inhabited. If the monsters reached their world, they were doomed. The station sent out a distress signal to their ship, and the soldiers turned the ship around. When they arrived, the planet was in ruins. No one was left, and the people had run out of time to escape. They had all perished on a distant planet, far away.

But there was a glimmer of hope. They had conducted research on a life rock from another dimension. They decided to take the portal and venture through. Upon arrival, they saw the monster again, staring at them. Without warning, it attacked. The group was split apart, but they used ropes to regroup and barely escaped the dimension, scratched and battered. The life rock was now ruled out as a solution. They had no new ideas and no one to turn to. Everything seemed lost.

How could they recover from such a blow? The universe seemed doomed, with nothing left to help them. The monsters began to rule once again. Meanwhile, a rebellion formed within the ranks of the monsters. One faction fought for peace, while another fought for survival. The peace rebellion sought out the aliens who had been lost, hoping to help. But when they found them, the aliens, in their desperation, began attacking the peace rebellion.

The survival rebellion soon followed, intent on confronting the peace faction. The aliens, caught in the middle, were paralyzed with fear. The peace side wasn't attacking them, which only added to the confusion. The survival side was advancing rapidly—faster than the man in the car and the monster combined. The aliens had no choice but to flee. The peace rebellion forced them onto a different planet, and the aliens were sent floating through space as the rebellion raged on.

As the aliens drifted, it became clear that the survival side was winning. Eventually, they collided with a planet, heading straight for the aliens. With no time to lose, the peace rebellion fell back and struck the planet, causing it to destabilize. The aliens, caught in the planet's gravity, were about to be crushed. In a last-ditch effort, they activated the rocket boots built into their armor and managed to land safely on the surface.

The war with the monsters raged on. There were no survivors, no stars left, nothing to rebuild. The universe had taken a fatal blow, and only the monsters remained. But a decision had to be made. The two factions of monsters reached an agreement: they would cease fighting each other until the universe was saved. They set off on a mission to find a rare gem that could restore life. It was located in a universe far from their own. Their journey began across the vast multiverse. Some universes were incredibly dangerous.

After nine months of searching, they discovered that the gem had been lost in another reality. To speed up their quest, they opened a portal that connected all the universes together. With this new shortcut, they split up to search for the gem. After nearly two years of searching, they finally found it. The leader of the group placed his hand on the gem, only to vanish into thin air.

There was a loophole in time: anyone who touched the gem would die. They now had to find a way to get rid of this time loop without perishing in the process. The group decided to hold a democratic vote to determine who would be the leader, and they moved forward with their plan. They traveled to an abandoned house and discovered a tool that allowed them to travel through time. However, the tool was a one-time use. They decided to use it, but soon realized that if they touched the gem, they would die. They were stuck in a time loop.

With no hope left, they remembered a person who had stayed behind. They needed to communicate with him to turn off the machine. But there was no way to contact him. The only option left was to return to the past, before they had entered the time loop. They managed to go back and turned off the machine, escaping the timeline. They decided to take the day off to recover.

Next, they needed to recreate the time-travel tool, but they had no idea how it worked. The smartest member of the group took charge, and after some effort, they managed to rebuild the tool—and even improved it. This new version had the ability to fix time loops. They used it to correct the timeline, and everything returned to normal.

With time flowing as it should, the leader of the group touched the gem again. This time, a flood of life surged into the universe, restoring balance. It was a magnificent sight.

They were proud of what they had accomplished.

THE FINALE
CHAPTER 9

Everything appeared normal, until they realized that EVERYTHING was back — even the monsters. This was a huge problem. The aliens were weary, and it was up to the monster saviors to help again. They had to eliminate the threat immediately. After discussing their options, they decided on a course of action. The aliens allowed them to borrow their weapons, and they thanked the aliens for their cooperation.

They set off on their journey back to the other universe. This was it — the final battle against the monsters. Once they arrived, they spotted the monster and began attacking from a distance. This was not going to be an easy fight. The monster retaliated, eliminating some members of the group. They were losing badly and had to retreat. They treated the injured soldiers, applying bandages, and regrouped. The leader then decided to ambush the monster.

This time, they had a plan. They went back out, armed with new tactics. They found a weak spot on the monster's back and launched a surprise attack, hitting it once. They repeated the process, trying to strike again. But this time, things didn't go as smoothly. The monster was quick to adapt and started countering their moves. They tried again, attacking from different angles, but they needed a way to catch it off-guard and deliver a decisive blow.

Finally, they devised a decoy ambush. The monster took the bait and started attacking the decoy, allowing the team to strike. They managed to wound the monster severely, bringing it to the brink of death. Just before it collapsed, the monster began to transform, shifting into a shape that resembled a picture. The group didn't think much of it and left the transformation behind, assuming it wasn't important.

They left the universe and reported back to the aliens about what had happened. Together, they decided to investigate the mysterious picture. However, there was little evidence of what the picture was or what it represented.

Determined to uncover the meaning, they began searching through various universes for clues. Despite their efforts, they found nothing concrete. They kept looking for things that could point to the meaning of the picture. However, all their searches in outer space came up empty.

Just when they were beginning to lose hope, one of the group members announced he was determined to find the clues, but he needed a team to help him. Four volunteers stepped forward to join him on the mission.

They began their journey, searching planets for any hints. On one planet, they found a note with the message: "The apple doesn't fall far from the tree." The group was confused, unsure of what this meant or how it related to their quest. They decided to check other nearby locations and found another clue, this one referencing a monster. But after that, they didn't find any more clues. They checked other solar systems and, during their search, made contact with a hostile creature. In self-defense, they managed to disarm it and began interrogating the monster. The creature revealed that a planet in a specific universe held "the Secret."

They were now faced with a new problem: which universe held the Secret? They returned to the monster and asked for more details. The creature was hesitant at first but eventually gave them the name of the universe. With that information, the group traveled to the universe in question and began searching for the Secret.

They scoured planet after planet, until they reached the last one. There, they found the Secret.

As they approached, a bubble appeared, floating around the Secret. When one of the team members touched the Secret, the bubble and the person both popped at the same time. The group was stunned. This strange encounter had led them to a book — but they were still confused about what had just happened.

Before they could react, there was a sudden explosion. Darkness enveloped everything, and nothing could be seen.

THE END

www.ingramcontent.com/pod-product-compliance
Lightning Source LLC
Chambersburg PA
CBHW071359200726
48294CB00004B/1226